STEPPIN' OUT

Jaunty Rhymes FOR Playful Times

poems by LIN OLIVER

illustrated by TOMIE dePAOLA

 Nancy Paulsen Books

Steppin' Out

When I open my front door,
There's a whole world to explore.

THE LIBRARY

"Welcome! Welcome! Come right in!"
The librarian says to me.
"Let's find some books for you to read.
I'll show you two or three.

"Here's one about a leopard
Who has a spotted tail.
Maybe one about a pirate
Or a mighty humpback whale?

"So many kinds of stories
Are there for you to find.
A book's a special treasure
To delight your busy mind."

A leafy tree, a buzzing bee,
A cloudy sky, airplanes that fly.

Shoe stores, fire trucks, cars that whiz,
Playgrounds full of laughing kids.

Step outside and poke around—
See the sights, hear the sounds.

Grab a hand and come with me.
Let's go see what we can see.

I walk all through the library.
At last, I pick a book
And settle down to open it
In the comfy reading nook.

When you're looking for a trip
For your imagination,
Check your local library.
That's this kid's recommendation.

Outside Sounds

Sirens wail, *aah-oo aah-oo*,
Cars go *beep beep beep*.
Trucks pass by, *ba-bump ba-bump*,
As birds go *cheep cheep cheep*.

The rain *drip-drops*, the bees they *buzz*,
The helicopters *whir*,
While over there, behind a bush,
I hear a kitty *purr*.

Woof woof, *honk honk*, and *clink, clank, clunk*—
So many sounds I hear.
Ding-dong, varoom, a big *ka-boom*,
It's a party for my ears!

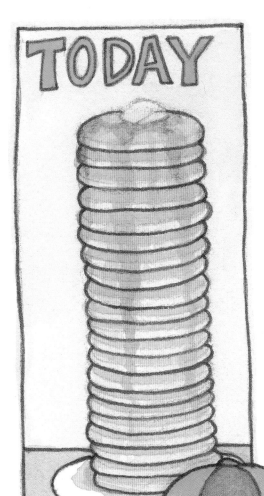

SUNDAY PANCAKES

Every now and then on Sunday,
My daddy's in the mood
To get a stack of pancakes—
Our favorite morning food.

We take a drive and find a spot.
I get a special seat.
We get a cup of something hot
And drink and talk and eat.

He tells a joke,
 I laugh *tee-hee*.
I love these times,
Just Dad and me.

Family Day

Aunts and uncles,
Cousins too,
We gather for a barbecue.

Lots of hugging,
Coochie-coo,
I can't wait until they're through!

The food comes out!
We shout hooray.
"Dig in, kids!" the grown-ups say.

They yak and yak
While we go play.
Lucky me, it's family day!

RAINY DAY AT GRANDPA'S

"It's raining cats and dogs out there,"
My grandpa says to me.
I grin at him and take his hand—
"Come on and follow me."

He looks surprised, but then I see
His old eyes start to flicker.
He climbs into his rubber boots
And hands me my red slicker.

I turn my face up to the sky
And open my mouth wide.
I catch the raindrops as they fall,
With Grandpa by my side.

He struts up to a puddle
And starts to splash and stomp.
I jump right in and join him
In a joyful, soggy romp.

There's nothing like a rainy day
When streets are seas of puddles,
And afterward a cup of tea
With snuggly Grandpa cuddles.

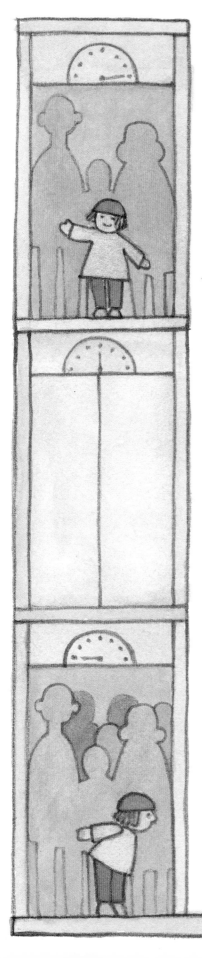

The Elevator

Going up!
I hear them say.
Step right in,
We're on our way.

Heads up, folks—
Today, I'm driving.
Seventh floor?
Yup, we're arriving.

Ding, ding, ding.
So now we're here.
More folks get in
And stand so near.

Going down!
They say to me.
I press ONE.
We're off—whoopee!

I like to ride
The elevator
Until I see . . .
THE ESCALATOR!

At the Car Wash

The vacuum sucks our cookie crumbs.
Next come the soapy suds.
Wash the windows, scrub the tires,
And lots of rub-a-dubs.

Rinse it clean with squirty water,
Dry it to a shine.
"Now, lookee there." My mommy smiles.
"Our car is mighty fine."

After dinner, in the bath,
With bubbles near and far,
I soap my arms and scrub my knees
Till I shine just like our car.

AT THE MALL

When we go shopping in the mall,
I look around and want it all!

Mommy says, "Now listen, honey,
Your dad and I aren't made of money.
You can pick out just one thing.
It's not a total shopping fling."

I can't decide what I should choose—
Puzzles, puppets, flashy shoes.

Then I see it over there:
The fuzzy pink koala bear.
"Oh, yes!" I shout. "I love that toy!"
And when we pay, I dance with joy.

I take that bear, lean down to kiss her,
And share her with my baby sister.

FOLKS ON THE STREET

I like it when I'm on the street,
And there are lots of folks to greet.

This one's bouncy, light as air.
That one's rolling in a chair.

This one's white and that one's brown.
This one's thin and that one's round.

This one's short, another's tall,
That one has no hair at all.

We're all so different, yet the same:
We're human beings—that's our name.

MY FIRST HAIRCUT

Hey, what is going on up there?
And who's that messing with my hair?
Are those scissors that I see?
And why is this sheet over me?

Mommy says it's haircut day.
I shake my head and say, "No way!"
She smiles and says, "My darling child,
Your hair is looking rather wild."

She holds my hand and we begin.
Snip, snip, snip—and then a trim.
I settle back into my chair,
And in no time, I have short hair.

Haircuts, kids, there's nothing to it.
It's kind of fun—I say just do it!

Super Market

Plop! I'm in the shopping cart,
Wheeling through the store.
My mouth begins to water
As we roll across the floor.

Look! See bright red strawberries,
And celery I can crunch,
And bags of pretzels on the shelf
For when I need a munch.

Peaches, waffles, pickles, plums—
Everything looks yummy!
When we get home, I'll taste it all
And put it in my tummy.

A BEACHY DAY

Sandals, sunscreen, beach balls too—
We head out to the sand.
I'll dig a hole to Timbuktu,
A shovel in each hand.

Then on my blanket in the sun,
I get to have a Popsicle.
I have to finish pretty fast
If I don't want a flopsicle.

You can't catch me, Mister Wave,
As you crash upon the shore.
Oh . . . I see you can't behave.
Okay, come splash me more.

A Sandbox Scene

While playing in the park one day,
A brown-haired kiddo came my way.
When he bent down and grabbed my shovel,
I knew that we were in for trouble.

"Hey, give that back! It's mine, not yours,"
I said, declaring sandbox wars.
Instead, he handed me a rake
And, just for laughs, a rubber snake.

I could have thrown a hissy fit,
But Mom said, "Try his toys a bit."
Know what? This sharing's not so bad.
I played with toys I never had.

Soon, he brought me his new ball.
I offered him my favorite doll.
Now, side by side, we share and play.
Can't wait to see him every day.

Playground Fling

The swing
Is a fling
In
The
Air.

The slide
Is a ride
For
Your
Rump.

The seesaw
Makes me yee-haw
Whoop
Dee
Doo!

LITTLE TREASURES

When you go out to take a walk,
Watch out for hidden treasure.
Scrunch down and notice little things—
A rock, a leaf, a feather.

You just might see a line of ants
Marching in a row,
Or flip a stone and find a bug
Wiggling to and fro.

Roly-polies, worms, and twigs
Are there for you to find.
So I suggest you take a walk—
Get up off your behind!

Dance Class

Listen up and hear the beat.
Start to sway, now move your feet.

Wave your arms and shake your butt.
Show the world how you can strut.

You've got rhythm—cut a rug,
Stomp and spin and jitterbug.

Twirl and leap and click your heels.
Show us how your gladness feels.

Hear the music, feel the flow,
Just get loose—now go, kid, go!

MY DAY

Now, you can call it day care
Or you can call it school—
No matter what you call it,
I think it's really cool.

With circle time and playtime,
Toys and games galore,
Stories, snacks, and friendships,
Who could ask for anything more?

When the day is over
And Nana comes to get me,
I say, "I want to go again,"
And she agrees to let me.

Day's End

Every night when I'm in bed,
Daytime memories flood my head.
Pizza pie,
Swings that fly,
Sunny beaches,
Juicy peaches,
Hooks and ladders,
Baseball batters,
Soaring kites,
And tickle fights.
Every day is full of fun,
And tomorrow is another one!

For Anarres and Elettra . . .
with love forever and ever—L.O.

In memory of my buddy Brontë,
who was the "dog-model" in my illustrations—T.DEP.

NANCY PAULSEN BOOKS
an imprint of Penguin Random House LLC
375 Hudson Street
New York, NY 10014

Library of Congress Cataloging-in-Publication Data
Names: Oliver, Lin, author. | DePaola, Tomie, 1934– illustrator.
Title: Steppin' out : jaunty rhymes for playful times / poems by Lin Oliver ; illustrated by Tomie dePaola.
Other titles: Stepping out
Description: New York, NY : Nancy Paulsen Books, [2017] | Audience: 1–3. | Audience: Pre-school, excluding K.
Summary: "A collection of nineteen original poems featuring toddlers exploring their world"—Provided by publisher.
Identifiers: LCCN 2016003360 | ISBN 9780399174346
Classification: LCC PS3615.L5864 A6 2017 | DDC 811/.6—dc23
LC record available at https://lccn.loc.gov/2016003360

Manufactured in China by RR Donnelley Asia Printing Solutions Ltd.
ISBN 9780399174346
1 3 5 7 9 10 8 6 4 2

Design by Marikka Tamura.
Text set in Engine.
The art was done in transparent acrylics on handmade Arches 140 lb.
cold press watercolor paper.